Ricky Ricotta's Mighty Robot vs. the Mecha-Monkeys from Mars

The Fourth Robot Adventure Novel by

DAV PILKEY

Pictures by

MARTIN ONTIVEROS

SCHOLASTIC INC.

New York Toronto London Auckland Sydney
Mexico City New Delhi Hong Kong Buenos Aires

For Felix
— D. P.
To Felix Salvador Ontiveros:
I can't wait to read this one to you!
— M. O.

No part of this publication may be reproduced, stored
in a retrieval system, or transmitted in any form or by any
means, electronic, mechanical, photocopying, recording, or
otherwise, without written permission of the publisher.
For information regarding permission, please write to:
Permissions Department, Scholastic Inc.,
557 Broadway, New York, New York 10012.

This book is being published simultaneously
in hardcover by the Blue Sky Press.

ISBN-13: 978-0-439-25296-6
ISBN-10: 0-439-25296-2

Text copyright © 2002 by Dav Pilkey
Illustrations copyright © 2002 by Martin Ontiveros
All rights reserved. Published by Scholastic Inc.

First Scholastic paperback printing, February 2002

Chapters

CHAPTER 1

The Big Mistake

One day, Ricky Ricotta
and his Mighty Robot were
playing hide-and-seek
in their yard.

"This game is too easy," said Ricky.
"Let's ride skateboards instead!"
    Ricky got his skateboard out of the
garage, but there was no skateboard
big enough for his Mighty Robot.

"I know," said Ricky. "We can use my parents' minivan!"

Soon, Ricky and his Mighty Robot were zooming down the street.
"This is fun!" said Ricky.

FONDUE
POND 1 MILE

But it stopped being fun
when they wiped out.
CRASH!

FONDUE POND JUST AHEAD

SPLASH!!!

FONDUE
POND

When Ricky and his Robot got out of the pond, they saw the smashed-up minivan.

Ricky's Mighty Robot put the
minivan back in the driveway.
"Maybe Mom and Dad won't
notice," said Ricky.

But they did.

CHAPTER 2

Big Trouble

Ricky's mother and father were not happy.

"Alright," said Ricky's father. "Which one of you boys squished our minivan?"

Ricky and his Mighty Robot
looked down at the ground.
They were very worried.

Finally, Ricky confessed.

"We both did," said Ricky.

"It was an accident."

"You boys were very irresponsible," said Ricky's father.

"Yes," said Ricky's mother, "and you will have to find a way to pay for the damage you have done."

CHAPTER 3
Major Monkey Hates Mars

Meanwhile, about 35 million miles away on the planet Mars, there lived a mean little monkey who was hatching an evil plan.

His name was Major Monkey,
and he hated living on Mars.
Mars was a cold, dry, and
very, very lonely place.

Major Monkey kept himself busy by building evil Robots and strange machines in his secret laboratory, but he was still lonely.

There was nobody to talk to. There was nobody to yell at . . . and, worst of all, there was nobody to be mean to. So Major Monkey decided to take over the planet Earth and enslave all of mousekind.

Major Monkey had watched Earth for many months. He saw other evil villains try to take over the planet, but they were always stopped by Ricky Ricotta's Mighty Robot.

BANANA JUICE

"I must get rid of that Mighty Robot!" said Major Monkey. "And I know just how to do it."

CHAPTER 4
The Trap

The next morning, as Ricky and his Mighty Robot walked to school, they tried to think of a way to pay for their mistake of wrecking the minivan.

"How many years will it take to buy a new minivan with my allowance?" asked Ricky.

Ricky's Robot used his super brain to figure out the answer. "Hmmm," said Ricky. "Only 259 years? Maybe we should think of a better plan."

Suddenly, a small spaceship
zoomed out of the sky. The top
of the spaceship opened up,
and a spacemouse peeked out.

"Help us! Help us!" cried
the spacemouse. "Mars is
under attack! We need your
Mighty Robot to save us!"

Ricky Ricotta's Mighty Robot could not turn away from someone who needed help. So the Mighty Robot followed the tiny spaceship all the way to Mars.

"Be careful up there!"
Ricky shouted.

CHAPTER 5

Betrayed

Ricky's Mighty Robot soon arrived on Mars. He saw a strange laboratory, but he did not see any evil villains.

The Mighty Robot flew closer to the laboratory. Suddenly, a giant metal hand reached out of the hillside.

It grabbed Ricky's Robot and
would not let go.

Ricky's Mighty Robot tried and
tried, but he could not escape
the grip of the giant metal hand.

Major Monkey looked up from
the tiny spaceship and pulled
a puppet off his hand.

"I tricked you! I tricked you!"
Major Monkey mocked. "Now
it is *YOU* who needs help!
Haw-haw-haw!"

40

Major Monkey pressed a button
inside his spaceship. Soon, three
giant Mecha-Monkeys rose from the
depths of the strange laboratory.

Major Monkey called out to his troops: "Mecha-Monkeys!" he cried. "It is time to take over Earth. Follow ME!"

CHAPTER 6

Major Monkey Makes His Move

Ricky was taking a spelling test when he saw the little spaceship return with three enormous Mecha-Monkeys.

45

"Hey," cried Ricky, "where's my Robot?"

"He got into a tight squeeze," laughed Major Monkey. "And he's never coming BACK— haw-haw-haw!"

"NOOOOO!" cried Ricky. But
there was nothing he could do.

Major Monkey flew through the streets of Squeakyville and ordered everyone on Earth to surrender.

"I'm the boss of Earth now," said Major Monkey. "And everyone must obey ME!!!"

CHAPTER 7

The Mouse from S.A.S.A.

That afternoon, Ricky sat in his bedroom missing his best friend.

"We are sure that your Robot will be O.K.," said Ricky's mother.

"Yes," said Ricky's father. "He'll find a way to escape. I just know it."

Soon, there was a knock on
the front door. It was a general
from the Squeakyville Air and
Space Association.

"We are going to send a space shuttle up to Mars to rescue your Mighty Robot," said the general. "He is our only hope."

"Hooray!" cried Ricky.

"And we need you to come
with us, Ricky," said the general.
"You know that Robot better
than anybody."

"Can I go?" Ricky asked his
parents. "Pleeeeease?"

"Well," said Ricky's father, "alright. But you must promise to be careful!"

"Hooray!" cried Ricky.

CHAPTER 8

The Space Shuttle

Ricky and his parents got into the general's car. The general turned on the rocket boosters, and they all flew straight to the Space Center.

"This is *so cool*!" said Ricky's father.

Soon, Ricky was sitting inside a giant space shuttle with three real astro-mice.

Ricky fastened his seat
belt, and off they blasted
into outer space.

When the shuttle arrived on
Mars, Ricky and the astro-mice
saw Major Monkey's laboratory.

They saw the Mighty Robot
trapped inside the giant metal
hand. But what could they do?

Suddenly, another giant metal hand reached out of the hillside and grabbed the space shuttle.

Then the strange laboratory
began to rise from the ground.

It rose higher and higher . . .

. . . until finally it stepped out of the ground. Major Monkey's laboratory had turned into a colossal Orangu-Tron.

The astro-mice inside the space
shuttle tried to open the emergency
exit door, but it was stuck. It could
only open halfway.

"I think I can fit through," said
Ricky.

Ricky squeezed his way out of the
space shuttle and headed toward
the laboratory.

CHAPTER 9

Ricky to the Rescue

The Orangu-Tron stomped its feet as Ricky bravely climbed up its giant arm.

Soon, Ricky found a doorway
in the Orangu-Tron's ear, and he
crawled inside the strange laboratory.

Once inside, Ricky looked around
the control center. He saw lots of evil
Robots and many strange machines.

Then, Ricky found the main power switch.

Ricky grabbed the switch and tried to turn off the power, but the switch was stuck. Ricky pulled and pulled on the switch.

ORANGU-TRON
MAIN POWER
SWITCH

Finally, Ricky was spotted by an evil Robo-Chimp.

"Destroy the intruder!" said the Robo-Chimp. "Destroy the intruder!"

The Robo-Chimp grabbed Ricky's
breathing tube and started pulling.
Soon, other Robo-Chimps joined
in. Harder and harder they pulled.

Then Ricky got an idea. He wrapped his breathing tube around the main power switch and held on tight. The Robo-Chimps pulled and pulled. Finally, the switch began to move.

The harder the Robo-Chimps
pulled, the more the switch moved.
Ka-KLANK!
Suddenly, the power for the
whole laboratory turned off.
"Hooray!" cried Ricky.

CHAPTER 10
Freedom

Outside, the Orangu-Tron lost all of its power. Ricky's Mighty Robot pushed his way out of the giant metal hand. He was free at last!

But inside, Ricky was in trouble. The Robo-Chimps rushed toward Ricky. "Must destroy intruder!" they chanted. "Must restore power!"

"HELP ME!" screamed Ricky
as the Robo-Chimps came
closer and closer.

KER-POW!

Ricky's Mighty Robot
punched a hole in the roof and
grabbed Ricky just in time.

78

Ricky pushed the SELF-DESTRUCT button with his tail. "Let's get out of here!" cried Ricky as the laboratory began to shake and crumble.

With Ricky in one hand and the space shuttle in the other, Ricky's Mighty Robot zoomed into space—just in time.

KA-BOOOOOOOOM!

"That takes care of Mars," said Ricky. "Now we have to save Earth!"

CHAPTER 11

Back to Earth

When they got back to Earth, Ricky's Mighty Robot spotted Major Monkey.

"What—what are *YOU* doing here?" asked Major Monkey.

"We're here to save Earth!" said Ricky.

"Oh, yeah?" said Major Monkey.
"We'll see about that!" He called his
Mecha-Monkeys and ordered them
to destroy Ricky's Mighty Robot.

Ricky's Robot put Ricky and
the space shuttle someplace safe.
Then the robo-battle began.

Ricky's Robot treated
the Mecha-Monkeys to
two servings of *punch* . . .

. . . and a *knuckle sandwich*.

Major Monkey was very upset.
"Alright, banana brains," he
shouted. "Quit monkeying
around! Let's see some action!"

CHAPTER 12

The Big Battle

(IN FLIP-O-RAMA™)

FLiP-
Hey, kids! You can animate the action by following these easy steps!

...O-RaMa

HERE'S HOW IT WORKS!

STEP 1
Place your *left* hand inside the dotted lines marked "LEFT HAND HERE." Hold the book open *flat*.

STEP 2
Grasp the *right-hand* page with your right thumb and index finger (inside the dotted lines marked "RIGHT THUMB HERE").

STEP 3
Now *quickly* flip the right-hand page back and forth until the picture appears to be *animated*.

(For extra fun, try adding your own sound-effects!)

FLIP-O-RAMA 1

(pages 97 and 99)

Remember, flip *only* page 97.
While you are flipping, be sure
you can see the picture on page 97
and the one on page 99.
If you flip quickly, the two
pictures will start to look like
<u>one</u> *animated* picture.

Don't forget to add
your own sound-effects!

LEFT HAND HERE

The Mecha-Monkeys
Attacked.

RIGHT
THUMB
HERE

The Mecha-Monkeys
Attacked.

FLIP-O-RAMA 2

(pages 101 and 103)

Remember, flip *only* page 101.
While you are flipping, be sure
you can see the picture on page 101
and the one on page 103.
If you flip quickly, the two
pictures will start to look like
<u>one</u> *animated* picture.

Don't forget to add
your own sound-effects!

LEFT HAND HERE

Ricky's Robot
Fought Back.

RIGHT
THUMB
HERE

RIGHT
INDEX
FINGER
HERE

Ricky's Robot
Fought Back.

FLIP-O-RAMA 3

(pages 105 and 107)

Remember, flip *only* page 105.
While you are flipping, be sure
you can see the picture on page 105
and the one on page 107.
If you flip quickly, the two
pictures will start to look like
<u>one</u> *animated* picture.

Don't forget to add
your own sound-effects!

LEFT HAND HERE

The Mecha-Monkeys Battled Hard.

RIGHT THUMB HERE

The Mecha-Monkeys
Battled Hard.

FLIP-O-RAMA 4

(pages 109 and 111)

Remember, flip *only* page 109.
While you are flipping, be sure
you can see the picture on page 109
and the one on page 111.
If you flip quickly, the two
pictures will start to look like
<u>one</u> *animated* picture.

Don't forget to add
your own sound-effects!

LEFT HAND HERE

Ricky´s Robot
Battled Harder.

109

RIGHT
THUMB
HERE

Ricky's Robot
Battled Harder.

FLIP-O-RAMA 5

(pages 113 and 115)

Remember, flip *only* page 113.
While you are flipping, be sure
you can see the picture on page 113
and the one on page 115.
If you flip quickly, the two
pictures will start to look like
<u>one</u> *animated* picture.

Don't forget to add
your own sound-effects!

LEFT HAND HERE

Ricky's Robot
Won the War.

114

Ricky's Robot
Won the War.

CHAPTER 13

Paying for Mistakes

Poor Major Monkey. His Mecha-Monkeys flew home to Mars, and he could not rule the world anymore.

"Boo-hoo-hoo!" cried Major
Monkey. "I've made a big mistake."

"Yes," said Ricky. "And now you
must pay for your mistake!"

Together, the two heroes put Major Monkey where he belonged: in the Squeakyville Jail.

"Thank you boys for saving Earth," said the general. "If there's anything we can do to repay you, please let me know!"

Ricky whispered in his Robot's ear. The Robot nodded his giant head.

"Well, sir," said Ricky, "we sure could use a new minivan."

"Alright," said the general.
"How many would you like?"

CHAPTER 14
Heroes

Ricky and his Mighty Robot flew back to the Space Center to meet Ricky's parents.

"Mom! Dad!" cried Ricky. "Look what the general gave us. A brand-new minivan!"

"Wow!" said Ricky's mother.
"We'll race you home!" said
Ricky's father.

So Ricky Ricotta and his Mighty
Robot raced the rocket-powered
minivan all the way home.

Soon, the whole Ricotta family was safe at home eating cheese pizza and drinking root beer.

"Thank you for rescuing each other today," said Ricky's mother.

"Yes," said Ricky's father, "and thank you for paying for your mistake."

"No problem," said Ricky.

"That's what friends are for!"

HOW TO DRAW RICKY

1.

2.

3.

4.

5.

6.

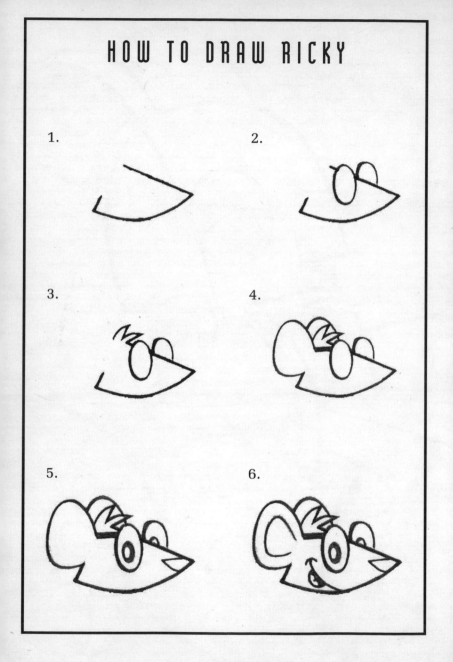

7.

8.

9.

10.

11.

12.

HOW TO DRAW RICKY'S ROBOT

1.

2.

3.

4.

5.

6.

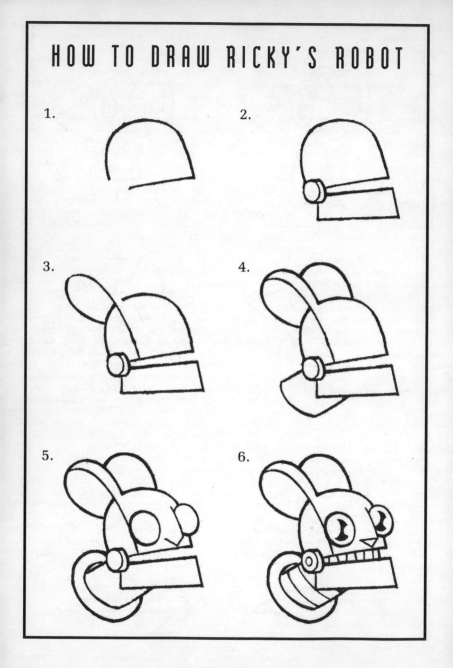

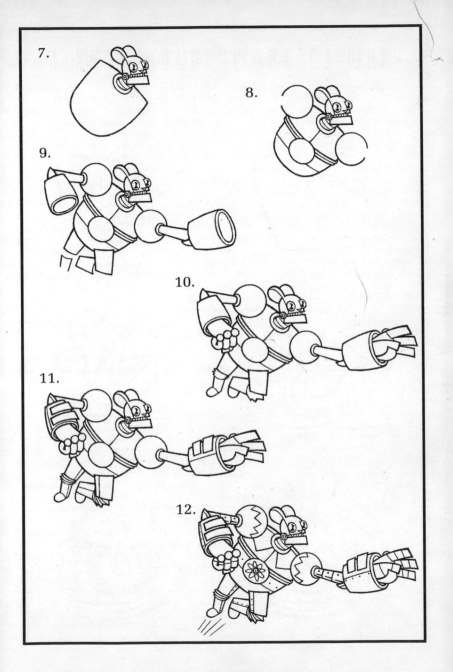

7.

8.

9.

10.

11.

12.

HOW TO DRAW MAJOR MONKEY

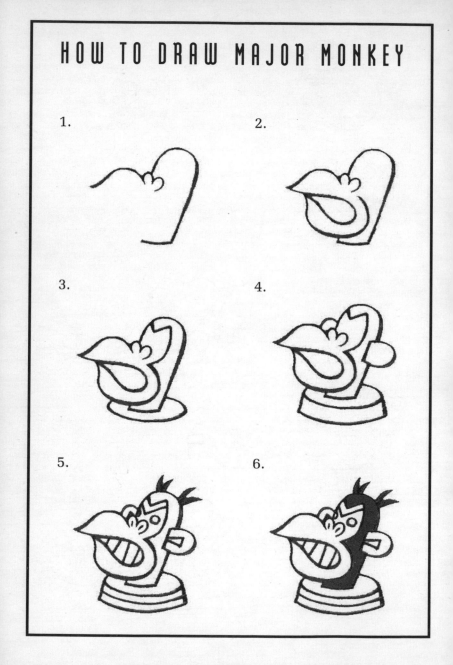

1.

2.

3.

4.

5.

6.

7.

8.

9.

10.

11.

12.

HOW TO DRAW A MECHA-MONKEY

1.

2.

3.

4.

5.

6.

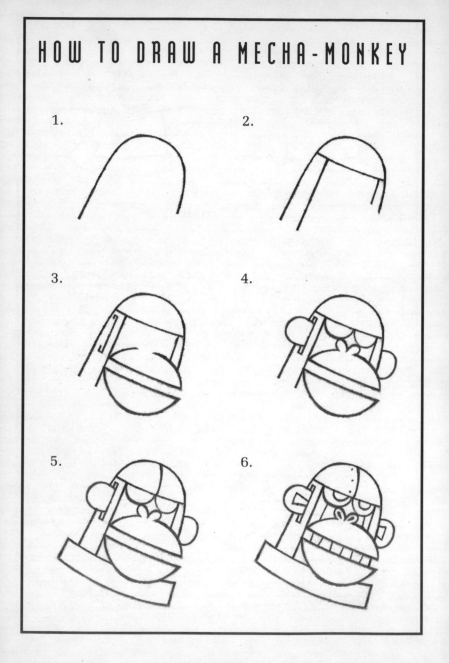

7.

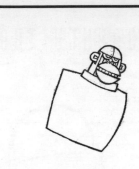

8.

9.

10.

11.

12.

HOW TO DRAW AN ORANGU-TRON

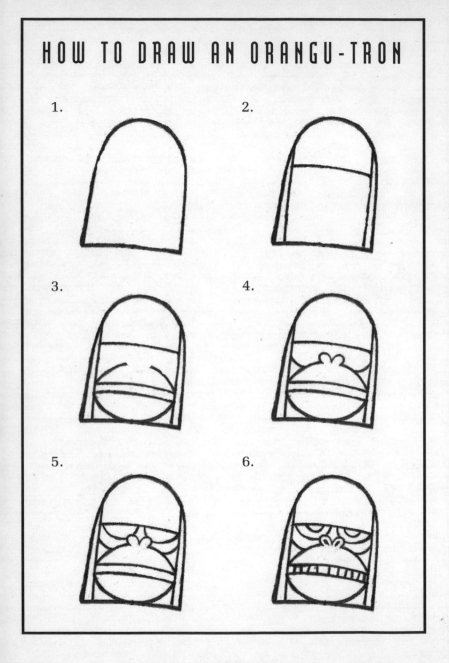

1.

2.

3.

4.

5.

6.

7.

8.

9.

10.

11.

12.

HOW TO DRAW A ROBO-CHIMP

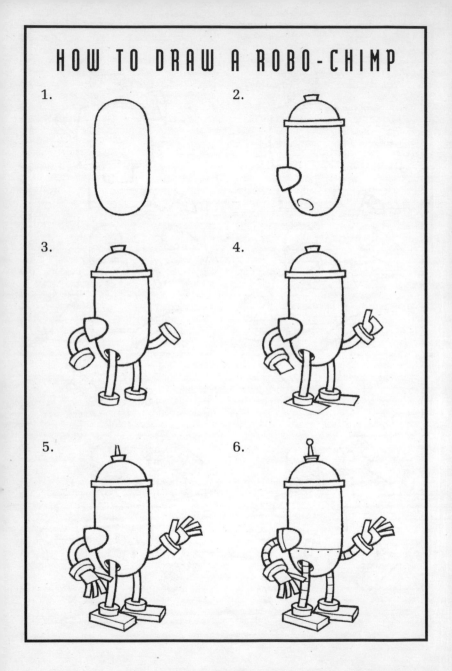

1.

2.

3.

4.

5.

6.

7.

8.

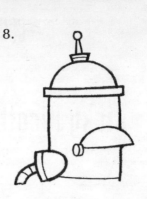

9.

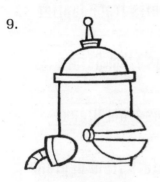

10.

11.

12.

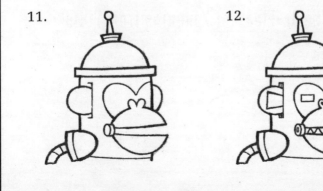

COMING SOON:

Ricky Ricotta's Mighty Robot

vs.

The Jurassic Jack Rabbits from Jupiter

The Stupid Stinkbugs from Saturn

The Uranium Unicorns from Uranus

The Naughty Night Crawlers from Neptune

The Un-Pleasant Penguins from Pluto

About the Author and Illustrator

DAV PILKEY created his first stories as comic books while he was in elementary school. In 1997, he wrote and illustrated his first adventure novel for children, *The Adventures of Captain Underpants*, which received rave reviews and was an instant bestseller—as were the three books that followed in the series. Dav is also the creator of numerous award-winning picture books, including *The Paperboy*, a Caldecott Honor Book, and the Dumb Bunnies books. He and his dog live in Portland, Oregon.

It was a stroke of luck when Dav discovered the work of artist **MARTIN ONTIVEROS**. Dav knew that Martin was just the right illustrator for the Ricky Ricotta's Mighty Robot series. Martin also lives in Portland, Oregon, and he can't wait to read this book to his newborn son, Felix.